MW01027553

Barney Wigglesworth
and the Party That Almost Wasn't

A BOOK ABOUT COOPERATION

Elspeth Campbell Murphy
Illustrated by Yakovetic

Chariot Books
David C Cook Publishing Co.

*Now you are the body of Christ, and each one of you is a part of it.
(I Corinthians 12:27, NIV)*

*Just as each of us has one body with many members, and these
members do not all have the same function, so in Christ we who are
many form one body, and each member belongs to all the others.
(Romans 12:4,5, NIV)*

DEAR PARENTS AND TEACHERS,

Barney Wigglesworth and the Party that Almost Wasn't is a story
illustration of these Scriptures. Their message is clear: We, as Christians,
all belong to the body of Christ and we all have different functions. And we
need one another. There's no room to say, "I'm the most important," or,
"I can get along without you."

While most children will not yet grasp Paul's comparison of the Church
to the human body, they've already felt some of the conflicts common
among members of the Body.

The story of the mice's party will help children understand how much
better life is when they follow God's plan, and cooperate and share—two
basic skills of friendship. The story is laying the groundwork for them to
understand how the Body of Christ functions.

Children know what it is to want to be first, best, and most important.
Yet, at the same time, friends are becoming more and more important to
children. They want to feel a part of the group and to get along with other
kids.

But why mice? It has been said that animal characters are really "kids
in fur coats." Children will readily identify with Barney, Gwendolyn, Tillie,
and Sam. But because animal characters are one step removed from real
life, the concepts of the book come across in a fun, nonlecturing,
nonthreatening way.

Now sit back and enjoy the party with your children!

Chariot Books is an imprint of David C. Cook Publishing Co.
David C. Cook Publishing Co., Elgin, Illinois 60120; David C. Cook Publishing Co., Weston, Ontario
BARNEY WIGGLESWORTH AND THE PARTY THAT ALMOST WASN'T

© 1988 by Elspeth Campbell Murphy for text and Yakovetic for illustrations.

Cover design by Dawn Lauck

First Printing, 1988 Printed in Singapore
93 92 91   5 4 3

Library of Congress Cataloging-in-Publication Data
Murphy, Elspeth Campbell
   Barney Wigglesworth and the party that almost wasn't. (Little epistles for kids)
   Summary: The party plans of Barney and his mouse friends are threatened until they decide to cooperate.
Includes a related Bible verse.
   [1. Cooperativeness—Fiction.   2. Mice—Fiction.   3. Parties—Fiction.   4. Christian life—Fiction]
I. Yakovetic, Joe, ill. II. Title. III. Series.
PZ7.M95316Bas 1988   [E]   88-4342
ISBN 1-55513-684-2

The trouble started when four of us church mice kids—Gwendolyn Scoot, Tillie Nibbles, Sam Scurry, and I (Barney Wigglesworth)—decided to have a little party.

Don't get me wrong. Having a party wasn't a bad idea. The trouble was deciding the best place to have it.

Gwendolyn thought we should have the party at her place. You see, the Scoot family has a mouse hole that opens into the Sunday school supply closet. So Gwen can get her paws on some really neat stuff.

You've heard the expression, "All that glitters is not gold"? Well, sometimes the stuff that glitters is— glitter. On Gwendolyn. Personally, I think she overdoes it a little. . . .

"A party isn't a party without costumes and decorations!" said Gwendolyn. "So *my* mouse hole is the best."

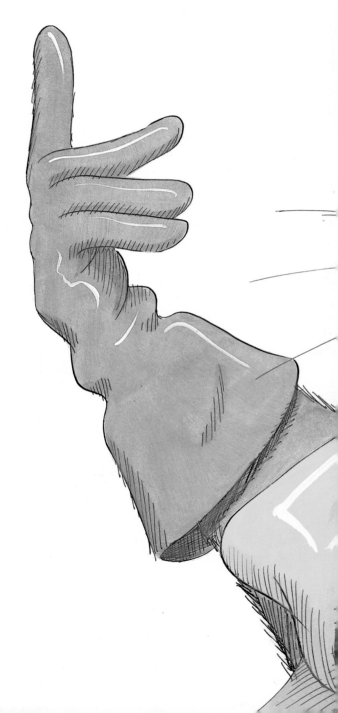

"A PARTY ISN'T A PARTY WITHOUT MUSIC!"
said Sam, who probably thought he was whispering.
"SO *MY* MOUSE HOLE IS THE BEST!"

Now, much as I like Gwendolyn, Tillie, and Sam, they're all wrong when it comes to mouse holes.

That's because we Wigglesworths have it best.

Our mouse hole opens into the church balcony. When I was practically still a baby, I figured out how to get onto the chandelier.

You've heard the expression, "The daring young man on the flying trapeze"? Need I say more?

"A party isn't a party without fun and games!" I explained. "So *my* mouse hole is the best."

I thought that would settle things once and for all.
But the argument kept on going:
"No, mine's the best!"
"No, mine's the best!"
"NO, MINE'S THE BEST!"
"No, mine's the best!"

"I'm going home!"

"See if I care. I'm going home, too!"

"I'M GOING HOME, AND YOU GUYS CAN'T COME!"

"So who wants to? I'll have my own party!"

"Oh, yeah? Well, I will, too. Who needs you guys?"

"Yeah, who needs you guys?"

"WHO NEEDS YOU GUYS?"

"Who needs you guys?"

So we all stomped on home to our own best-mouse-holes to have our own little parties.

After a while, I realized my party wasn't going very well. I mean, sure, I had my trapeze. But I had no one to swing on it with me. Plus, I didn't have any decorations . . . or party food . . . or music. . . .

I went to look for Gwendolyn, Tillie, and Sam.
   And guess what! Gwendolyn, Tillie, and Sam were
coming to look for me!
   We started planning the party again.
   And this time we got it right.

First we went to Gwendolyn's place and got ourselves all decorated up.

Then we went to Sam's place, and he showed us how to play the piano.

Then we went to my place and flew through the air with the greatest of ease.

And then we went to Tillie's place where she had—
are you ready for this?—a giant cookie table! When
Tillie said, "OK, you guys, come to the table," we
pulled up our stools and—*ate the table*!

"Tillie, this cookie is absolutely fabulous!" cried Gwendolyn. "A party wouldn't be a party without it!"

Tillie blushed with pleasure. "But a party wouldn't be a party without your decorations, Gwen!"

"Or Sam's music," added Gwendolyn.

"OR BARNEY'S GAMES," said Sam.

I said, "Everybody brought something different to the party, and we all worked together. But you know the most important thing we brought? Ourselves! Because, when you get right down to it, a party isn't a party without mice!"

Gwendolyn, Tillie, and Sam all nodded their heads happily and said, "Mumff rightff!"

THE END